DEPARTMENT OF THE ARMY TECHNICAL MANUAL

DEPARTMENT OF THE AIR FORCE TECHNICAL ORDER

TO 31-3-16

INTERNATIONAL
MORSE CODE
(INSTRUCTIONS)

DEPARTMENTS OF THE ARMY AND THE AIR FORCE
SEPTEMBER 1957

Technical Manual
No. 11-459
Technical Order
No. 31-3-16

DEPARTMENTS OF THE ARMY AND
THE AIR FORCE

Washington 25, D. C., *17 September 1957*

INTERNATIONAL MORSE CODE
(Instructions)

* This manual supersedes TM 11–459, 9 August 1945, including C 1, 19 May 1952

CHAPTER 1
INTRODUCTION

1. Purpose and Scope

a. This manual is a guide for the instruction of students who are learning and acquiring skill in *audible* International Morse Code. It describes methods for teaching code, evaluating student progress, and conducting practice exercises.

b. Forward comments on this publication direct to Commanding Officer, United States Army Signal Publications Agency, Fort Monmouth, N. J.

2. References

References pertaining to subjects within the scope of this manual are listed in the appendix.

3. Code Language

a. International Morse Code used with radio-telegraphy communication is made up of short and long pulses of sound. The short sounds are *dits*, and the long sounds are *dahs*. The code should be thought of in terms of *dits* and *dahs*, never a and dashes.

b. Combinations of dits and dahs form t letters of the alphabet, the 10 numerals, a punctuation marks. The dits and dahs that prise a particular character should not be co but the peculiar sound and rhythm of the con tion, as such, must be memorized.

c. The code phonic sound of the alphabe numerals is shown in figure 1. Except wh forms the final syllable of a character, a dit i tracted to di, the *t* becoming lost in the *d* syllable that follows.

4. Military Lettering and Phonetic phabet

a. The radio operator must be able to cop received code on paper quickly and accur At slow speeds this is done with pencil, but at faster than the hand can write, the typewri

LETTER	INTER-NATIONAL MORSE CODE	PHONIC SOUND	LETTER	INTER-NATIONAL MORSE CODE	PHONIC SOUND
A	· —	di DAH	N	— ·	DAH dit
B	— · · ·	DAH di di dit	O	— — —	DAH DAH DAH
C	— · — ·	DAH di DAH dit	P	· — — ·	di DAH DAH dit
D	— · ·	DAH di dit	Q	— — · —	DAH DAH di DAH
E	·	dit	R	· — ·	di DAH dit
F	· · — ·	di di DAH dit	S	· · ·	di di dit
G	— — ·	DAH DAH dit	T	—	DAH
H	· · · ·	di di di dit	U	· · —	di di DAH
I	· ·	di dit	V	· · · —	di di di DAH
J	· — — —	di DAH DAH DAH	W	· — —	di DAH DAH
K	— · —	DAH di DAH	X	— · · —	DAH di di DAH
L	· — · ·	di DAH di dit	Y	— · — —	DAH di DAH DAH
M	— —	DAH DAH	Z	— — · ·	DAH DAH di dit

NUMBER	INTER-NATIONAL MORSE CODE	PHONIC SOUND	NUMBER	INTER-NATIONAL MORSE CODE	PHONIC SOUND
1	· — — — —	di DAH DAH DAH DAH	6	— · · · ·	DAH di di di dit
2	· · — — —	di di DAH DAH DAH	7	— — · · ·	DAH DAH di di dit
3	· · · — —	di di di DAH DAH	8	— — — · ·	DAH DAH DAH di dit
4	· · · · —	di di di di DAH	9	— — — — ·	DAH DAH DAH DAH dit
5	· · · · ·	di di di di dit	0	— — — — —	DAH DAH DAH DAH DAH

TM459-1

Figure 1. Phonic sound of International Morse Code.

A ALFA (AL FAH)	B BRAVO (BRAH VOH)	C CHARLIE (CHAR LEE)	D DELTA (DELL TAH)
E ECHO (ECK OH)	F FOXTROT (FOKS TROT)	G GOLF (GOLF)	H HOTEL (HOH TELL)
I INDIA (IN DEE AH)	J JULIETT (JEW LEE ETT)	K KILO (KEY LOH)	L LIMA (LEE MAH)
M MIKE (MIKE)	N NOVEMBER (NO VEM BER)	O OSCAR (OSS CAH)	P PAPA (PAH PAH)
Q QUEBEC (KEH BECK)	R ROMEO (ROW ME OH)	S SIERRA (SEE AIR RAH)	T TANGO (TANG GO)
U UNIFORM (YOU NEE FORM)	V VICTOR (VIK TAH)	W WHISKEY (WISS KEY)	X XRAY (ECKS RAY)
Y YANKEE (YANG KEE)	Z ZULU (ZOO LOO)	1 WUN	2 TOO
3 THUH-REE	4 FO-WER	5 FI-YIV	6 SIX
7 SEVEN	8 ATE	9 NINER	0 ZERO

THE UNDERLINED PORTION OF THE ALPHABET DE-NOTES ACCENTED SYLLABLE(S). TM 459-2

Figure 2. Military lettering and phonetic alphabet.

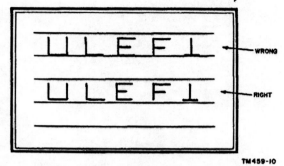

TM459-10

Figure 3. Right and wrong lettering on ruled paper.

used. Figure 2 illustrates the prescribed method of printing letters and numerals. In addition, figure 2 gives the phonetic name for each letter in the alphabet and the pronunciation of the names and numerals.

b. The following points are prescribed for military lettering:

(1) Make U's with square corners to prevent them from looking like V's.

(2) Place a short line through Z to prevent confusion with the numeral 2 or 7.

(3) Place a slanted stroke through the numeral Ø (zero) to distinguish it from the letter O.

(4) Underscore the numeral 1 to avoid confusion with the letter I.

(5) Make E with two strokes, not three or four. This will save time.

(6) Carefully print the numeral 5 to prevent confusion with the letter S.

(7) When ruled paper or message blanks are used, print slightly *above* the line. This prevents confusion of U with 11, 1 with I, and F with E when the horizontal base stroke is made over the ruling on the paper (fig. 3).

CHAPTER 2
TEACHING METHODS

5. General

a. The phonic or sound system is the most effective and most flexible method of teaching code. The student should be taught to think of the signal at all times as a pattern of sound. It may be some time before a student is able to resist the temptation to count dits and dahs; he must constantly try to hear each signal as a complete and distinct unit of sound. Eventually, recognition of every signal will be practically instantaneous and he will be able to copy code as fast as he can print it on paper.

b. Methods of teaching code will depend largely on the type of equipment used. Some equipment is used solely for the purpose of familiarizing students with the code characters; other types of equipment are used to further increase the proficiency of the students in receiving code.

c. All students should be taught to copy code by hand for speeds up to 18 groups per minute (gpm). The typewriter is used for speeds greater than 18 gpm. Intercept procedures and format require all copy to be made by typewriter. This necessitates considerably less practice in copying by hand and proportionately more practice on the typewriter.

6. Tape Method

a. The tape method of instruction involves the use of equipment that automatically reproduces audible code practice signals previously recorded in ink on paper tape. Code signals may be presented at varying speeds depending on the teaching pattern being followed. The tape method is particularly adaptable in teaching large groups.

b. Code practice tapes are made of ⅜-inch wide rolls of paper with inked lines which, when used with appropriate equipment, produce signals of the International Morse Code. The tapes are prepared for beginners and advanced students and may be obtained through normal supply channels.

c. The code signals may be reproduced through speakers or headsets.

7. Recorder-Reproducer Method

a. The recorder-reproducer method involv use of equipment that records code, voice, noise, or combinations thereof on metallic magnetic plastic tape, and phonograph (disks), and reproduces through speakers or sets.

b. The characters of the code may be pre at varying speeds with different patterns. method can be used for introductory or high lessons.

c. It can also be used for providing cod tude tests.

8. Code-Voice Method

a. The code-voice method involves the us oscillator or similar code training set which pr the dits and dahs under control of the ope key. The students may receive these through speakers or headsets. When transi signals through a speaker, the instructor m the instruction by orally introducing each ch after the signal is given (similar to the re reproducer method).

b. The code-voice method is suitable for te code when personal instruction is available an elaborate code practice equipment is lackir

c. The code-voice method is used only tc beginners the basic code characters. For greater than 5 gpm, the code characters a without voice. An occasional call back of p groups will aid the beginner in recognizi error.

d. Correct timing by the instructor is an imp factor in the code-voice method. The i between the signal and announcing the letter never be less than 3 seconds and, if it can be av not more than 4 seconds. An interval that long is preferable to one that is too short pause between the name and the next signal be 1 second. It must not be less than 1 and not more than 2 seconds.

AC

CHAPTER 3
CODE INSTRUCTIONS

Section I. RECEIVING CODE

9. General

Equipment should be arranged to enable personnel to receive code under the best possible conditions. Proper lighting and spacing are important. Leave enough space at each table position so that the student can rest his arms comfortably.

10. Practice Code Sheet

a. General. The practice code sheet is simple to use. It provides a continuous record of the beginner's progress, and affords practice printing in groups of five characters, the most commonly used code group. The sheet contains 100 double squares in each block; *b* below illustrates a method in which they may be used.

b. Instructions. The instructions contained in (1) through (6) below explain how to use the code practice sheets (fig. 4). Each subparagraph explains a numbered indication on figure 4; the numbers on the figures correspond to the subparagraph designations.

    (1) Instruct students to fill in the heading on every sheet before receiving code.

    (2) The student upon hearing the code signal, prints the character it represents in the *top* square.

    (3) At the end of the lesson, the instructor calls off the correct characters, and the student prints in the *bottom* square the characters he missed.

    (4) The bottom square will be left blank if the character in the top square is correct.

    (5) The top square is left blank if the student did not attempt to print the character. The correct character is printed in the bottom square when the instructor identifies it.

    (6) Tally the errors in the right hand margin after each group of blocks.

c. Progress. As the student progresses, he will be able to recognize his improvement by checking the bottom squares. Thus, the practice sheet serves as a quick reference regarding student's progress and indicates the characters that caused the most trouble.

d. Types of Code Runs. The practice sheet in figure 4 shows two types of code runs. Notice that every letter or figure in the top run appears twice in succession. This is known as a run of doubles and is intended to accustom the student to the sound of each character early in practice. A typical run of *singles* is shown in the lower portion of the practice sheet. The practice sheet may also be used on runs of singles without identification at a speed of 5 gpm. Errors are corrected when the run is over and the characters are identified by the instructor.

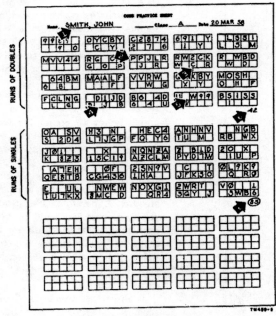

Figure 4. Code practice sheet.

TM400-2

11. Beginner's Lesson

a. The pattern in which the code characters are sent to beginners may vary as follows:

    (1) All the letters of the alphabet and the 10 numerals are taught (in any sequence) from the beginning of the practice.

    (2) Letters of the alphabet and the 10 numerals are divided into lessons. The early lessons consist of letters of simple code characters, and the later lessons consist of the more complex letters and numerals.

    (3) When using the touch-typing system (par. 29), letters of the alphabet and the 10 numerals may be divided into lessons corresponding to the letters on the typewriter keyboard. The numerals selected may correspond to each finger as used in the touch-typing system, or numerals may be sent as a group in later lessons.

b. Beginner's lessons should be presented with the characters in runs of doubles and then in singles (fig. 4). After several lessons of doubles and singles, the lessons should combine five mixed characters in a group. These groups make it impossible for students to anticipate the next character. They also provide experience in receiving enciphered groups.

c. Procedure signs (prosigns) may be introduced after all the code characters have been taught. (See ACP 124(B).) However, students must not be confused by running prosigns in with the regular signals. As a general rule, one prosign should be sent at the end of every 25 signals.

d. Practice exercises resembling actual messages (both cipher and regular words) should be used at speeds greater than 5 gpm.

e. Students should be instructed that if any character is not recognized at once, they should not stop and attempt to count the character because this will mean the loss of several succeeding characters. The student should leave the space blank and continue to copy.

f. Advanced students should be able to receive code through an interfering background of other signals. Therefore, background music or other rhythmic sounds should be used to aid high-speed operators. These sounds do not distract the students but rather relieve the tedium of the code signals. The rhythm produced by background music also helps the student develop fast and even keyboard strokes.

g. Procedure messages should be introduced as soon as the student has attained proficiency in receiving the alphabet and numerals.

12. PARIS Standard

a. To standardize practice and test tap 5-letter word PARIS is used to establish th ber of elements in each group at every spee For example, a speed of 20 groups per mi established by setting tape pulling equipm regulating hand-sent transmission to a spee will send the word PARIS exactly 20 tim(minute. This standard also applies to all used in army schools on basic code learning (Some tapes still in use employ the CODEZ ard.)

b. All code receiving practice is based on acter sent at 20 PARIS groups per minute courage the student from counting dits and This is slow enough to make the signal re able as one sound unit and fast enough to the character *from falling apart* during the tr sion. At this speed, the following relat exists between the elements of the code cha

    (1) The dit is the unit of length.

    (2) The dah is equal to three dits.

    (3) The space between the dits and dahs the character is equal to one dit.

    (4) The space between characters is e three dits (applies only to code transmitted at a speed of 20 gpm or

    (5) The space between groups is eq seven dits (applies only to code transmitted at a speed of 20 gpm or

c. In order to give the student time to re the signals, the space between the complet acters and groups is longer during early p at lower speeds. As the students' skill inc the space between characters is gradually de until recognition is almost instantaneous.

13. Code-Voice Practice Runs

a. This course consists of 24 hours of inst as follows: 20 lessons should consist of 20 h code practice, leaving 4 hours of the cour for orientation, review of military printing, te the phonetic alphabet, discussion of the m portant prosigns, etc. Some students wi reach the 5 gpm speed in the allotted time, few will be ready for higher speed practice. fore, a code practice schedule should be to meet individual conditions.

b. Code practice material for the cod method is broken down into 20 lessons witl lesson consisting of 3 runs—one of doubles, singles, and one at 5 gpm, as shown below.

LESSON 1

Doubles
```
5 5 D D N   N 4 4 G G   S S 7 7 Z   Z 1 1 M M   Ø Ø U U T
T P P H H   C 3 3 9 9   Y X X V V   W W R M I   I F F A J
K K B B H   C J J L L   Y O O 8 8   2 2 E E Q   6 6 F D Ø
J 4 4 8 8   Q Q 7 7 B   B F F 2 2   U U 1 1 G   G L L Ø Ø
```

Singles
```
W O K D L   Z Ø F S N   O 1 K D O   B Ø 6 L L   S 7 9 Q S
C 9 4 A G   P G J U 1   G Z 3 Y U   I S F E 9   W N U G E B
Ø R X O 7   8 G 2 U T   6 I H P 4   N P E C W   9 7 M V B
6 2 6 U 3   Ø 4 Z U Ø   J V T J B   I 7 F A 8   J W A 5 2
```

5 GPM
```
B O W 9 C   B A 7 J O   C D 8 A O   J 7 X 8 P   9 Y T 2 M
Ø D N E 9   V G O V U   G D L D W   Q 5 Q 5 E   S 4 L K 1
6 K U F 4   M 2 X T Z   2 G Y Q X   G 3 H Y S   H B V Z N
L 1 G 8 A   7 U R J 4   3 8 J C R   H Z F 5 A   I R I P K
```

LESSON 2

Doubles
```
9 9 Y Y P   P A A M M   S S R R Z   Z I I V V   W W C C 6
6 X X O O   5 5 H H T   T E E K K   3 3 N N 8   8 2 2 C C L
1 1 N N 6   6 9 9 T T   O O A A B   B M M 4 4   K K U U L
L X X E E   H H Ø Ø P   P 3 3 F F   Y Y R R I   I Q Q J J
```

Singles
```
X K 4 Q J   5 9 U M 3   K 8 G D D   C G 2 3 1   V B D T T
O W X R F   P G C Ø 6   M X 9 8 5   8 C Q D A   8 L Y J M
C F H Q X   7 5 3 Z 1   E R 1 R 7   W V I 3 4   R H G Q J
B 5 1 O L   M A S E P   8 5 Y 5 K   7 L X N Y   2 Y X Z Y
```

5 GPM
```
L O E I G   9 T Ø B Ø   1 K M 8 F   R 1 C K M   N F T Z H
S N W U P   W 6 2 I 3   V 3 X 5 P   4 E Y 7 L   2 K E S T
7 S Ø Y G   C I 5 7 U   B M K 8 G   3 R Z 1 O   L 4 W A F
9 F K 3 J   E H 8 F 6   D U 4 9 C   I L X X 1   V O H C M
```

LESSON 3

Doubles
```
V V S S Z   Z G G 7 7   W W D D 5   5 1 1 H H   Z Z 6 6 R
R G G 4 4   Q Q P P 9   9 B B I I   K K V V 8   8 3 3 W W
M M F F D   D 2 2 L L   5 5 X X E   E S S Ø Ø   U U O O Y
Y A A C C   7 7 T T J   J N N R R   L L F F G   G A A 1 1
```

Singles
```
E W H H N   O D O 4 K   F R B 4 Y   9 S H I N   2 1 V P 3
M 1 N K H   T F M E A   Q B C A S   Z P Z K 2   T L V I T
J 2 Y X Z   1 X N Y 9   Ø Y N N Q   6 1 A 1 G   X B 5 1 0
7 8 Z 7 B   Y W V I 3   R 1 R 7 4   P X C R F   Ø L E M A
```

5 GPM
```
Q Ø D Z U   P P W A 2   T 9 Q X Ø   V R Y N 5   P D H B E
S Z L G I   N 4 J 8 6   T 5 J M 6   W 7 2 Y B   3 O N Q A
6 Q Ø F 7   9 S G 1 I   3 5 H R K   Ø Q H U W   E 4 W X G
1 N L R 8   D V E A 8   Ø P 4 J Z   T K C K U   M O I R Y
```

LESSON 4

Doubles:
```
6 6  E E  8 8  4 4  3 3   P P  2 2  T T  7 7  V V  Y Y  Z
X H  H S  8 O  O N  9 9   I P  I 5  5 Ø  Ø K  K U  U G  C C  L B  B K  M
D D  J J  Q Q  F N  1 1   Q Q  A A  7 7  K R  R Z  G G  P L  L M
I X  X H  H F  F 1  1 6   6 9  9 Ø  Ø W  W Z  Z P  P P  M M
```

Singles:
```
Y 2 5 E G   S V N O L   D M X 9 8   G C Ø 6 L   B 3 T
B D T T E   B S G A 8   I A M B W   M 5 9 U D   K 4 Q
O J W 8 5   7 F A 8 I   V H 8 D P   3 Ø 6 1 J   H 6 2
K Z 9 F 2   5 N P E I   A H P 4 6   U O I J R   5 4 2
```

5 GPM:
```
A N E C Z   T N 5 M G   6 D 2 I 9   H S 8 4 K   N Q V
1 Y M X P   3 O 2 B S   D 8 J O F   L C R Z 9   I P V A
G Ø A J 4   B L Y W B   7 V J U 2   G R Z 9 1   P X 2 N
X 9 J 4 Y   L D Z M E   H F O 6 5   G Q S C V   R Q N
```

LESSON 5

Doubles:
```
D D  T T  J J  3 3  5 5   Y Y  8 8  E E  S S  V V  N N  O
2 B  B D  U U  4 4  M M   4 1  1 L  L G  G Z  Z I  I P  J
V V  D T  U 9  9 6  6 H   H C  R A  A Q  Q W  W 8  8 P  3
2 X  X T  T S  S B  B 5   5 R  R 7  7 N  N E  E F  F Ø  Ø
```

Singles:
```
Z 3 8 C H   Q K S 7 R   Q G Ø 3 G   C J U I G   C L H
S 9 Q S V   1 I K U W   U K 4 U O   C Z Ø F Z   Y K D M
N H W W S   T A C L Q   X V Q O 4   R N P P F   R E I V
G Y T 3 W   3 P V L K   E 4 O D O   T P 5 E X   W I V
```

5 GPM:
```
B Y 2 7 W   6 M J 5 T   6 8 J 4 N   I G L Z S   E B H
5 N Y R V   Ø X Q 9 T   2 A W P E   U J Ø D F   M C A W
1 X X 1 I   C 9 4 U D   6 F 8 H A   C 3 K F 9   F A H S
O 1 Z R 3   G 8 K M B   U 7 5 A I   C G Y Z S   7 T S
```

LESSON 6

Doubles:
```
O O  Y Y  P P   8 8  I I  1 1   O O  6 6  R R  F F  L L  Y
V C  C D  D S   S 2 2  K K  9 9  T T  E E  U W  W Ø  Ø N  5
J J  H H  Q Q   4 4  M M  3 3   Z Z  X U  U 7  7 G  G I  I
A F  F 9  9 R   R X  X 8  S W   W Q  Q 6  6 J  J N  N N  I
```

Singles:
```
P H J 2 O   G 8 R K 5   T P 1 U 7   A C Y F 7   6 5 N
U 2 H 9 N   J G C Q W   Y G I U T   Z 5 V M 6   E 4 E
N B 3 Q I   1 6 J 4 K   C J W K 3   I 7 S 4 8   8 K L
M O B 5 X   B T M Ø W   2 S 1 Ø F   L H C 9 L   1 2 4
```

5 GPM:
```
B 5 3 E Q   4 S Ø K 1   A W C W 4   3 7 O 8 L   P Ø 8
X 1 2 Z O   2 Q 6 N T   7 5 Q B 1   A N Ø S G   A D R
F Q S R 6   O F D Z T   L 9 T C 5   2 H U Z L   H E M
J R K B C   X I N W D   K U G 2 9   S H 6 F 9   V E 1
```

Doubles

```
X  D D  V V  1     1 Ø  Ø K  K     7 7  S S  U     U Z  Z 3  3     Y Y  5 5     O
W  O 4  J 4  P     O C  C E  K     2 2  B B  A     U A  C M  G     G P  H F     K E
I  J J  6 6  3     O D  8 8  X     X L  4 4  U     U B  C B  A     A N  N 7     W Ø
C  E Q  Q 3  3     D D  V V  L     L M  M B  C     B A  A N  N     7 Y  Y Y     Ø
```

Singles

```
9  U Q  D F  S     F H  D W  R     Y 5  9 P  O     X V  E L  Z     S Z  Y 3  R
Z  1 R  Z X  Y     2 3  D Z  G     Q V  Ø M  X     N 9  D A  6     T E  X 7  B
U  T D  B M  U     9 5  J Q  4     K 8  9 X  M     6 0  C A  3     I V  W 0  R
J  I U  J C  I     E P  N 4  P     H A  5 8  W     J 8  A F  7     U 6  2 6  T
```

5 GPM

```
T  X 1  J 3  P     K V  R V  Z     E I  O U  3     D 4  G 6  J     8 W  P A  M
3  Y U  8 T  L     T 7  5 B  H     C X  4 F  V     M Y  I J  1     I 7  U A  O
W  D Q  G 5  O     4 P  Ø 6  H     P 3  M E  8     6 O  L 5  Y     A F  3 G  9
3  U H  I D  F     T M  5 G  7     T Q  W 9  Z     X L  Z 6  8     Q K  M K  4
```

Doubles

```
2  5 5  9 9  R     R H  H T  T     S S  I I  2     2 Z  Z 1  1     3 3  U U  W
U  W R  R T  T B   7 7  4 4  Q     Q J  J O  X     2 9  9 1  1 K   K M  M U  H
2  Z Z  C C  B     B Y  Y 2  2 D   I X  X A  N     A P  P E  J     5 5  8 8  V M
K  V L  L S  S     Ø Ø  G G  D     D 6  6 N  N     F F  E E  J     J R  R M  M
```

Singles

```
Ø  C A  T 7  F     M E  R V  S     Q 9  S Ø  F     Ø Z  L D  K     Y G  3 Z  G
8  X N  Y B  5     1 0  2 K  L     V P  3 O  D     O 4  E S  W     H D  H N  Q B
7  H A  Z M  1     3 0  A O  Ø     V O  4 F  4 M   Q 5  7 D  M     H D  S L  O A
2  Ø 6  G K  V     B 4  E 9  W     I 2  W T  R     X P  Y C  5     N L  O A  C
```

5 GPM

```
P  S Z  F V  C     2 W  1 9  R     Y T  W E  R     2 V  8 I  J     S X  H J  P
V  X 3  U H  8     B C  N N  4     1 A  K J  C     D Ø  B E  V     2 Y  R N  L 7
L  C X  6 Ø  X     K Z  T L  U     5 P  L 7  A     S I  I 3  T     Y A  Ø U  D K
K  L Ø  N 2  S     4 B  O 1  6     C W  H W  A     G 7  D X  9     Q 1  I D  P
```

Doubles

```
V  N N  P P  V     V G  G F  F     W W  A A  Y     Y U  U Q  Q     4 4  O O  6
B  6 8  8 3  3     T T  7 7  D     D S  S I  I     X X  9 9  2     2 K  K B  B
A  C C  Z Z  5     5 Ø  Ø H  H     1 1  L L  C     C U  U 9  9     L L  Ø Ø  G N
L  G H  H F  F     P P  Q Q  S     S 4  4 7  7     E E  3 3  D     D I  I N  N
```

Singles

```
7  T 8  N 6  J     9 N  4 H  W     E F  P X  T     B 8  G 1  6     5 I  2 G  Y
I  Z B  9 U  S     L V  7 E  K     X G  J P  Y     M T  9 A  U     3 U  C 4  5 1
R  Z Ø  2 7  H     5 Q  I Y  7     6 8  J Q  F     N Ø  L Z  C     D L  X V  R
8  2 L  1 X  N     Y D  H R  8     K 1  B P  S     S Q  K I  E     R J  U 2  R
```

5 GPM

```
N  X 4  B M  A     P N  D 7  6     5 V  4 E  N     Y B  2 Y  M     R 8  O 8  H
7  8 S  M Q  9     2 L  J Z  E     K 9  M T  R     O E  U C  7     C G  1 B  V F
G  2 F  W E  Ø     I W  J J  4     I H  O R  3     V K  S 8  Y     S O  Q V  8 E
M  5 3  P R  J     N G  Z G  F     3 O  5 Q  Y     Q J  Z Y  5     0 6  8 E
```

Doubles
```
J J   2 2   R R   Y Y   5 5   A A   W W   O L   O Y   8 8   K K   B B   T
M 1   7 7   Z Z   X X   V V   V M   M Ø   L L   4 Y   A A   B B   D N   N X
I 1   7 7   P P   Z Z   2 2   3 3   Ø Ø   1 1   U U   A O   B O   H H   6
W 9   9 9   R R   Q Q   8 8   D K   K K   1 1   U U   O O   C C   C 6   6
```

Singles
```
R Q   B C   A G   T S   W H   H D   N O   D O   4     E K   L V   P     3 B   5
I U   B J   C D   3 Z   G 2   L 6   K A   Y F   Ø F   8 Z   W J   H Q   P 9   S A   7 I   F E
5 T   J T   D R   U 6   2 6   V 6   6 Ø   7 C   5 G   8 W   9 X   M J   Q     4     K     M
Y 2   7 R   B 1   R 3   I V   W     6     Ø     8     9
```

5 GPM
```
M 3   P B   6     Ø P   4 O   5     G Q   D O   A G   U 7   I 1   6     Z L   X
W A   T 7   G 9   5 M   F C   D V   I F   U S   9 K   3 F   Q Ø   I E   8 V   2 D
W W   Y R   1 4   N W   2 B   8 H   U 3   X P   K J   M K   Q S   J L   B Ø   7 D
K A                 N   C     8 H         F                 H X           L   Y     L
```

Doubles
```
E E   V V   G G   F F   M M   K K   B B   H H   5 5   L L   S S   J
R 9   X T   X N   Z O   Z D   W U   U Q   Q 4   8 8   E P   7 F   6 3
1 1   T Y   T G   C A   H H   2 2   A A   4 E   4 Ø   Ø P   N N   Q Q
I Y   T G   N G   O A   D X   X M   M E   E     7 7   P P   P
```

Singles
```
8 G   I F   U U   3     Z H   Q U   1     R Q   1 5   B X   F J   X   Y D   U S
Q O   J D   C P   3 L   Z Q   F C   H 7   V P   D W   3 B   R Z   E Y   2 3   X 1   O 5
R N   6 B   Ø H   S Z   Q D   F T   K     V N   M W   B 6   T G   9 N   K N   X     5
4 R   7     H     Z     D     T I   1     W     Z W   V           J
```

5 GPM
```
X S   U D   Y     X E   J     F     X     B A   5 1   Q R   1     U Q   H Z   3     U F   I W
1 Y   T P   C D   M E   K 6   L X   7 2   D J   W 5   9 Y   U O   I Y   X 3   H Q   T N   K Ø   W U
3 A   2 S   B     E I   6     X Y   6     Ø V   L Z   S 8   4 L   H L   G     N 9   1 Ø   8
I 5   Z     B     E     I     6     Y     J
```

Doubles
```
K K   2 2   Y     Y     8     B     L L   C C   3     G G   6 6   1 1   W
I V   J D   D U   Ø A   8 A   T 4   4 F   9 F   9 M   S K   Z Z   J J   J D
U U   J J   U O   A X   8 A   1 8   Y 9   F 9   S     K 6   Z Z   L L   3 3
B C   C     O     X     8     4     4     9     S     6     Z 2   E
```

Singles
```
4 M   W W   K     A T   Q 3   X     I U   9 5   W     A 7   L K   E     C P   T
4 I   5 9   3 Ø   V 8   Z H   C 4   J E   9 V   F 6   U 2   C 6   W M   C Q   T 2
G 6   U Ø   Ø 1   7 N   H G   R L   Y O   L Z   F     D 2   X I   M E   D S   Z
V J   8     Ø     J     9     L     8     S           J Y   6     E     B
```

5 GPM
```
2 S   Q     A     1     8     H     A     P     Ø     D     E     W     7     K X   R     N     M
P 1   M W   R M   8 5   9 Ø   Y L   A C   A X   G B   J S   L F   P 4   Q 9   A J   M 1   G T
K W   W B   R N   6     2     Q     E     R     7     3 9   T 6   M Y   H
W M   B         6       Ø   2     X     E                 N       9     A
```

Doubles
```
M   I I   G G   P P   7 7   R R   Q Q   N N   W W   V V   H H   T T   5 5   L
5   L N   N T   T W   W 8   8 R   R R   I I   O O   Y P   P Q   Q H   C C   K K   9 9   L
N   S S   3 3   F F   U U   5 R   J J   Ø Ø   O Y   Y X   X D   C 2   2 B   B 9   7
T   7 M   M Z   Z E   E H   H A   A 1   1 6   6 Y   G G   V V   D 5   5 E   E L   L 7
```

Singles
```
O   U 3   M H   N R   X K   F 7   W E   E D   Ø P   A H   V 8   1 A   Q S   2
E   N 7   G M   M O   9 4   P 7   L J   K G   A A   Y Ø   9 P   8 R   M 1   P
N   P P   T Y   1 A   T Q   3 3   F S   4 Ø   X C   E L   X 8   2 5   M W   W M K
9   X S   A 9   Ø J   6 G   9 N   4 R   7 B   R E   Q M   2 Ø   6 N   B M   W
```

5 GPM
```
9   K 4   P 2   I N   Ø 5   1 N   C W   M P   G W   L N   B Z   T O   D J   J
E   Z 4   T 2   B S   C F   O G   9 Z   7 L   L U   6 6   E 4   F 5   D V   J H
J   U F   I G   3 I   K 5   C 5   P W   V 9   H H   Q H   Z 3   X S   U N   D A
R   6 M   4 H   L 7   W E   T R   5 O   9 4   P J   K G   A A   3 R   N A   T
```

Doubles
```
R   7 7   1 1   R R   S S   Y Y   N N   9 9   F E   A A   O O   K K   B B   H
V   H V   V 4   4 I   I T   T W   W C   C X   X 2   2 Q   Q P   P Z   Z H   G
I   U U   3 3   J 8   6 6   J J   D D   Ø Ø   M M   K K   M M   Z Z   8 8   G L
R   G 5   5 J   J F   F Ø   Ø 4   4 T   T P   P 2   2 3   3 C   C U   U L   L
```

Singles
```
X   J J   D O   T Z   B N   L W   G P   M W   C N   1 5   Ø N   1 2   P 4   K
J   H V   D 5   F 4   E 6   6 U   L 1   7 Z   9 G   O F   C S   B 2   T 4   Z
4   O D   U S   X 3   Z H   Q H   H 9   V W   P 5   C 5   K I   3 G   I F   U
5   T A   N R   3 A   A G   K J   P 4   9 Ø   5 R   T E   W 7   L H   4 M   6
```

5 GPM
```
8   S G   Y O   H Q   U 3   M H   X K   F 7   D K   E B   7 I   1 D   2 U   C
4   J I   A Q   S J   8 Ø   1 Z   8 7   Y X   3 T   9 M   U Y   Y 6   I E   L
G   Y B   8 Z   5 G   C R   Q Y   A 1   8 1   S O   L V   Ø 7   L D   2 X   6
V   Q B   O I   Ø U   D 8   V V   8 Z   R C   N R   J E   9 E   F F   H P   K
```

Doubles
```
I   1 1   D D   R R   6 6   B B   H H   9 9   S S   O O   Y Y   N N   I I   7
5   7 A   A V   V W   W E   E Q   Q X   X E   E 2   2 S   S 9   9 T   T 4   4
B   M M   R R   F F   N N   G G   K K   7 7   Ø Ø   J J   3 3   A A   Y Y   P
Ø   P 8   8 5   5 X   X U   U D   D Z   Z Q   Q L   L V   V H   H C   C B   B
```

Singles
```
1   C U   2 D   1 I   7 B   E K   D 7   F K   X H   M 3   U Q   V O   Y G   S
0   L E   I 6   Y Y   U M   9 T   3 X   Y 7   8 Z   1 Ø   8 J   8 Q   A I   J
3   6 X   2 D   L 7   Ø V   L O   S 1   8 1   A Y   Q R   C G   5 Z   8 B   Y
I   K P   H F   F E   9 E   J R   N C   R Z   8 V   V 8   D U   Ø I   O B   Q
```

5 GPM
```
U   J K   8 3   2 E   Z R   B 3   T 5   D V   H S   C F   O L   P C   6 O   Q
N   4 2   O X   K Y   4 T   2 B   C W   M P   7 V   I F   Q 8   Ø 6   D N   R
P   5 Ø   5 1   N N   9 G   6 B   V W   Z N   K 1   T T   D Z   H B   7 R   4
K   O G   T W   C Q   B C   2 U   F E   9 E   C R   Z 8   V 3   9 5   I 4
```

Doubles
```
1  1   O  O   9    9 I  I   W  W   8  8   J  J   9    9 3  3 2  2   Q    Q  S
C  4   4  V  V   6 1 6   T  T   D  Z   W  W  Y  O  Y   O  R   M  L   P  7  P   G  E   H  U
K  K   N  N  B   1  X  X   I  I  4  4   3  Ø  Ø   K  K  Y   N  N  R   R  C  C   8  8  9  9   M  M  U
5  A   A  B    X  X   4  4  3   K  K   N  N   8  8  9  9   M  M  U
```

Singles
```
X  W   2  3  N   Q  Z  6  7  Ø   3  P  Ø  A  V   7  I  R  8  R   B  R  T
6  E  C   8  1  S  Y   T  I  U  Y  H  L   H  G  6  V  E  S   Z  2  K  4  5   N  E  L  8
E  Ø   S  V  N   F  M  4  9  L   A  G  F  D  V   W  K  7  3  6   Z  L  L  A
O  Ø   J  6  Y  N   X  L  I  Z  A   C  5  7  H  V   9  Ø  8  Z  4   E  L  A
```

5 GPM
```
B  G   T  R   B   R  8  R  I   7   V  A  Ø  P  3   O  7  6  Z  Q   N  3  2
Y  4   L  E   N   5  4  K  2  Z   E  V  D  6  G  G   H  Y  U  I  T   S  1  8
7  6   8  L   Z   6  3  7  8  Ø   V  D  F  G  5   L  Z  I  L  X
D  C   A  L   E   4  Z  8  Ø  9   V  H  7  5  C   A  Z  I  L  X   N  Y  6  J
```

Doubles
```
W  W   Q  Q   2    2  5  5   J  J   V  V   E  E   S   S  L  L   U  U   A  A   G
Ø  7   7  R  Y   R   H  H  1  1   P   P  D  D  Z  Z   I  I  F  F  O   6   9  B  B   1
X  X   Y  Y   R  N  J   N  5  5   H  H  W   S  S  G  G  A   Ø   Ø  7  7  O   O  2   9  L  L
K  I   I  J   J   3  3   R  R  H  W   W  Q  Q  A  A   P  P  D   D  Z   Z  L   L
```

Singles
```
Ø  9   5  S  3   O  Ø  8  X  M   P  Ø  K  U  U   7  T  3  F  O   X  M  W  W
T  Y   C  2  Y  R   Q  K  H  Q  V  V   P  9  A  8  V  K   A  L  J  P  G   1  I  W  K
D  M   J  C  R  2   K  Q  4  Ø  W  G   Z  Q  4  V  T  H   L  S  S  P  4  E   R  2  W  R
1  M   E  9  2   F  B  1  J  G   8  G  6  T  H   3  5  P  E  O   R  2  W  R  N
```

5 GPM
```
D  F   W  M   X   O  F  3  T   7   U  U  K  Ø  P   M  X  8  Ø  O   3  S  5
9  1   W  I   1   P  G  J  S  A   V  K  8  9  P  Z   V  Q  H  K  Q   Y  2  C
5  W   K  W   R   G  4  J  P  L   K  V  4  Q  Z   W  Ø  4  Q  K  F   R  C  J
D  J   N  R   2   O  E  P  5  3   H  T  6  G  8   G  J  1  B  F   2  9  E
```

Doubles
```
X  X   4  4   F   F  E  E  U  U   2  2  B  B  C   C  M  M  8  8   Y  Y  V
T  M   M  K  K   C  C  D  2  2  U  J   J  Ø  Ø  1  1   3  3  U  O  U  7   7  Y  Y  L   5
9  9   6  6  N   N  D  D  T  T   4  4  Z  Z  V   V  O  O  H  R  R  B   P  P  L
Q  F   F  G  G   8  8  I  I  E   E  X  X  S   W  W  H  H  B   B  L  L
```

Singles
```
Z  B   J  T  Y   B  7  C  M  X   F  5  Q  9  2   O  N  I  X  S   Y  U  I
H  U   N  M  U  M   1  T  I  C  X  X   N  A  U  D  R   Q  N  B  2  P  1  4   J  H  3
U  5   F  E  M  D   U  P  M  1  2  6   V  4  G  A  V   W  C  Y  F  5  2   R  O  E
D  S   5  3  D   K  N  K  A   Ø  F  Y  O  1   8  G  F  2  4   F  W  P
```

5 GPM
```
5  F   I  U  Y   S  X  I  N   O   2  9  Q  5  F   X  M  C  7  B   Y  T  J
D  B   3  H  J  R   P  1  2  B  Q  W   R  D  U  A  N  V   X  C  I  T  1  U   U  M  N
9  N  C   E  O  J  3   N  5  Y  I  U   V  A  G  4  I  K   4  A  M  P  3  R   M  E  F
X  C   2  O  3   N  L  I  U  L   J  B  7      S  1  S  R   D  3  5
```

A(

Left margin column:
```
C F 5 T
B Y 7 D
X 6 E O
Ø O K 6
D 9 5 D
Ø T D 1
T A Q N
5 D 9 J
Z H U D
```

Doubles
```
8  8  U  U  O    O  L  L  B  B    3  3  D  D  J    J  V  V  S  S    M  M  G  G  E
E  X  X  I  I    P  P  Y  Y  W    W  Z  Z  6  6    7  7  5  5  Ø    Ø  F  F  4  4
1  1  T  T  Q    Q  2  2  A  A    9  9  R  R  H    H  C  C  K  K    9  9  4  4  G
G  V  V  D  D    P  P  7  7  A    A  N  N  S  S    8  8  Ø  Ø  W    W  E  E  Q  Q
```

Singles
```
L  9  G  Y  7    D  C  1  A  Z    I  V  Q  P  J    Q  H  9  P  E    C  U  6  5  M
9  W  Z  E  S    N  M  B  X  Q    5  P  P  T  Ø    Q  K  V  J  X    M  4  S  L  K
B  D  Ø  7  C    G  5  F  O  P    Q  P  X  T  3    M  R  T  Y  F    S  4  Ø  8  8
O  I  E  X  6    K  N  K  A  6    Ø  F  Y  O  1    8  G  F  2  4    F  W  P  J  J
```

5 GPM
```
M  5  6  U  C    E  P  9  H  Q    J  P  Q  V  I    Z  A  1  C  D    6  Y  G  9  L
K  L  S  4  M    X  J  V  K  Q    Ø  T  8  P  Q    Q  X  B  M  N    S  E  Z  W  9
8  8  Ø  4  S    F  Y  T  R  M    3  T  X  P  Q    P  O  F  5  G    C  7  Ø  1  O
J  J  P  W  F    4  2  F  G  8    1  O  Y  F  Ø    6  A  K  N  K    6  X  E  I  O
```

LESSON 20

Doubles
```
X  X  H  H  R    R  J  J  I  I    M  M  U  U  B    B  3  3  2  2    K  K  Z  Z  T
T  6  6  1  1    5  5  F  F  O    O  L  L  Y  Y    C  C  W  W  D    D  7  7  1  1
8  8  2  2  T    T  Q  Q  C  C    V  V  3  3  Y    Y  I  I  5  5    H  H  R  R  B
B  F  F  U  U    Z  Z  K  K  X    X  6  6  M  M    J  J  G  G  A    A  L  L  P  P
```

Singles
```
I  7  4  E  A    O  9  H  E  Y    R  H  L  6  V    8  W  D  H  8    7  K  W  W  Ø
R  U  3  T  Y    5  L  9  B  3    O  4  N  V  Q    D  S  Z  6  3    I  2  G  W  H
1  B  J  T  7    R  D  C  C  X    7  U  6  K  M    1  V  J  S  H    N  A  G  B  1 2
H  Ø  T  Z  Z    2  R  I  5  Y    2  T  U  Q  L    Ø  B  8  G  A    Z  G  N  9  2
```

5 GPM
```
Ø  W  W  K  7    8  H  D  8  W    V  6  L  H  R    Y  E  H  9  O    A  E  4  7  I
H  W  G  2  7    3  6  2  S  D    Q  V  N  4  O    3  B  9  L  5    T  Y  3  U  R
1  B  G  A  N    H  S  J  V  1    M  K  6  U  7    X  C  C  D  R    7  T  J  B  I
2  9  N  G  Z    A  G  8  B  Ø    L  Q  U  T  2    Y  C  5  I  R  2  Z  Z  T  Ø  H
```

14. Method of Testing and Grading

a. The instructor must be familiar with the progress of each student. When a student is having difficulty, the instructors must endeavor to diagnose the trouble and assist in overcoming it.

b. Speed tests should be scheduled regularly. When a student is able to present solid copy at a given speed, he should be given a test and his papers graded. A standard speed qualification requires the student to receive code without error for 3 consecutive minutes out of 5.

c. When the paper is graded, it should be returned to the student so that he can know the characters that give him the most difficulty.

Section II. SENDING CODE

15. General

Students should normally start sending code as soon as they qualify at a speed of at least 5 gpm on all letters and numerals. A minimum of one-third of the entire code practice time should be spent in transmitting. This time may vary, since some students require more time than others to acquire correct sending habits.

16. Hand Key

Before students can send properly, the hand key must be properly adjusted and the contacts correctly spaced. Figure 5 is a detailed drawing of a hand key, indicating the parts referred to in the following adjustment instructions:

a. The *spring tension screw*, just in front of the key button, controls the amount of tension exerted

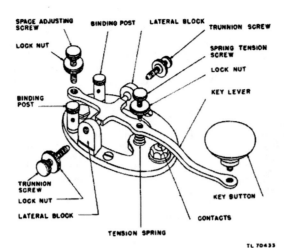

SPACE ADJUSTING SCREW — BINDING POST — LATERAL BLOCK — TRUNNION SCREW — SPRING TENSION SCREW — LOCK NUT — LOCK NUT — KEY LEVER — BINDING POST — TRUNNION SCREW — LOCK NUT — LATERAL BLOCK — TENSION SPRING — CONTACTS — KEY BUTTON

TL 70433

Figure 5. Hand key.

upward on the key. The tension allowed will usually vary with individual operators. Too much tension will force the key button up before the dahs are completely formed; spacing between characters will be irregular, and dits will not be clearly defined. If the spring tension is very weak, the characters will run together and the space between characters will be too short.

b. The gap between the contacts, regulated by the *space adjusting screw* at the back of the key should be set at one-sixteenth inch for beginners. This measurement does not apply to every key and is a matter of personal preference. As students progress, further gap adjustment may be made to suit their sending speed. Contacts that are too close have an effect similar to weak spring tension, and contacts that are spaced too far have the same effect on sending as too much spring tension.

c. The final adjustment of the key is the sidewise alinement of the contact points. The *trunnion screws* at either side of the key control this alinement. If they are too tight, the key lever will bind and if they are too loose, the contacts will have a sidewise play. Contacts must be kept clean to prevent scratchy signal. When the sidewise alinement is correct, no further adjustment normally is required.

d. Proper adjustment of the contacts of the hand key should be made before practice sending begins. A satisfactory method of adjusting the gap between contact points can be made as follows:

    (1) Tighten the space adjusting screw until the contacts are just closed.

    (2) For early sending practice, turn th adjusting screw counterclockwise revolution.

    (3) Turn the screw counterclockwis fourth revolution for correct gap s sending practice above 7 gpm. (nick or pencil mark on the adjustin will aid in estimating the amount o

17. Position of Hand at Key

a. Take a position at the key that is natu comfortable. The following pointers on p of the hand and arm have been helpful t radio operators:

    (1) Lay arm along the table in a natur tion so that the fingers reach t button without straining.

    (2) Place the tip of the first (index) fi the tips of the first two (index and fingers on the top of the key butto far edge or just overlapping the fa Keep the fingers away from the parts of the key to avoid a possible

    (3) Place thumb and third (ring) or (little) fingers on the right and le of the knob lightly to guide and slapping the key.

    (4) Allow the large muscles of the for do most of the work when transi Putting strain on the smaller mu the wrist or hand will result in *gla* a condition of temporary paralysis by overfatigue.

    (5) Make a downward motion with th the wrist acting as a fulcrum betw forearm and the hand.

b. Figure 6 illustrates a good hand position operator prefers to send with his index fi

Figure 6. Proper hand position at key.

14

A

Figure 7. Proper hand position at key, side view.

Figure 8. Position of hand at key.

top of the button, using the thumb and middle finger as guides at the side. Compare figure 6 with the hand illustrated in figure 8. (The shirt sleeve has been removed in all illustrations to show how the arm is supported on the table.)

c. In figure 7, notice that the index finger slightly overlaps the edge of the key button.

d. In figure 8 the operator touches the top of the key button with the tips of the first two fingers. The thumb and two fingers are at the sides of the button to guide and control it.

18. Preliminary Sending Practice

a. After the student has checked the position of his hand at the key, he should begin transmitting a series of dits to develop timing and to get the feel of the key. Students should concentrate on spacing the dits equally. In this preliminary practice, students should not send characters at random but should send from some prearranged lesson. Students should send as smoothly as possible, gradually increasing speed as muscles limber up. After students have achieved a rhythmic, steady swing, the instructor should check their transmission. This can be done by having the students try a series of I S H 5 in any order.

b. After students have mastered sending dits satisfactorily, they should send a string of dahs, preferably imitating a good model. Students should concentrate on regular spacing and remember that the space between dahs should be no longer than the space between dits. When the instructor is satisfied that the dahs are rhythmic and properly spaced, students should send a series of T M O Ø in any order.

c. Students should begin to combine dits and dahs with simple characters such as R, K, A, N, and V. When they have mastered the basic character differences, practice should be continued to develop speed.

d. Whenever possible, students should send to each other to permit comparison.

19. Difficult Characters

A skilled operator can increase his speed if his sending practice emphasizes certain difficult characters. Therefore, give special attention to students' practice on the following characters: 3, 4, 6, C, 1, 2, H, 5, Y, V. These signals should appear more frequently than others during practice, and the instructor should make sure that they are formed correctly from the beginning of practice.

20. Practice Material

When students learn code by the tape or record method, their first sending practice should be based on the characters and speed learned in the beginner's lesson. For additional sending practice at higher speeds, the following six exercises have been weighed to include a majority of the more difficult characters. These exercises will be of assistance to the instructor who uses his own sending as a model for student practice.

```
E  E  E  E  E    T  T  T  T  T    M  M  M  M  M    A  A  A  A  A    D  D  D
O  O  O  O  O    D  M  E  O  T    A  D  M  O  E    T  T  O  M  E    O  A  M
A  T  E  D  D    A  T  O  A  D    I  I  I  I  I    N  N  N  N  N    S  S  W
R  R  R  R  R    U  W  U  W  U    W  W  W  W  W    R  N  N  N  S    I  R  K
N  W  R  U  I    I  G  R  G  N    U  S  R  U  U    I  U  R  N  S    K  K  9
Z  Z  Z  Z  Z    G  G  G  G  K    B  B  B  B  B    F  F  F  F  F    9  Z  F
B  K  F  K  9    G  7  F  7  7    F  Z  P  K  P    ø  ø  9  ø  G    K  J  J
9  F  B  9  B    7  V  V  V  V    P  P  ø  P  ø    7  7  8  V  P    J  J  L
Q  Q  Q  Q  Q    V  V  ø  V  P    Q  ø  J  Q  V    8  8  8  8  8    P  L  8
Q  V  Q  7  P    P  X  X  X  X    J  7  J  V  ø    Y  Y  Y  Y  Y    L  L  L
5  5  5  5  5    X  L  5  H  5    H  H  H  H  H    5  X  8  H  8    X  H  4
X  L  8  Y  Y    H  C  C  C  C    8  5  L  X  Y    6  6  6  6  6    Y  4  2
2  2  2  2  2    C  2  1  C  1    1  1  1  1  1    6  6  6  6  6    4  6
3  3  3  3  3    6  3  4  1  3    6  1  4  2  6    3  4  3  3  C    6
2  C  1  3  3    C  3  .  1  3
```

```
9  8  3  2  4    P  L  F  R  B    R  E  I  N  P    2  5  7  9  2    G  A  Z
H  Q  W  F  A    2  3  1  7  2    W  M  H  S  T    G  B  C  K  C    3  9  8
I  B  K  N  G    6  9  3  ø  5    4  5  3  4  3    U  B  P  L  F    3  9  6
2  7  2  5  3    Z  H  K  G  G    K  S  K  L  P    3  1  9  8  1    F  Y  J
V  X  M  V  H    4  5  1  9  ø    C  U  L  O  N    Z  N  G  K  D    7  6  7
U  Y  Y  B  X    W  B  H  P  V    6  ø  9  3  6    Y  X  C  Y  W    V  I  D
Q  C  G  V  H    9  2  6  5  7    P  D  P  R  F    P  U  X  Z  S    ø  9  3
L  L  C  Y  V    R  L  O  F  J    6  3  1  2  7    C  V  H  H  J    Q  C  J
1  5  3  5  4    J  H  Y  Q  V    W  J  U  X  H    5  4  6  1  3    1  6  5
C  Q  H  J  X    3  2  6  3  1    Z  U  Q  I  B    5  ø  1  3  8    Y  Y  C
Q  L  C  P  H    1  ø  2  8  4    X  Y  H  Y  2    L  C  X  H  P    8  4  6
Y  C  J  X  7    X  V  F  P  W    ø  5  ø  2  L    V  J  Q  X  V    L  0  4
1  4  4  2  7    ø  4  6  8  8    Q  C  Q  J  L    5  ø  1  4  1    L  C  X
Q  H  C  L  X    3  8  7  7  8    Z  R  C  S  G    4  8  4  3  6
```

```
B  B  B  B  B    B  6  A  6  B    B  D  B  X  B    C  C  C  C  C    C  Y  Y
C  H  C  K  C    A  A  N  A  A    N  A  I  A  M    D  D  D  B  D    E  D  E
H  H  H  H  H    H  5  A  5  H    H  S  H  V  H    E  E  B  T  E    P  I  A
1  1  1  1  1    L  J  N  J  L    1  9  1  4  1    F  F  F  P  F    5  F  8
J  J  J  J  J    J  1  1  1  J    J  W  J  U  J    9  9  5  9  9    5  9  4
L  L  L  U  L    G  P  P  P  G    L  W  L  R  L    5  5  5  5  5    5  4  J
5  5  5  5  5    M  M  D  M  M    D  G  Z  G  R    2  2  2  2  2    2  J  F
2  H  2  2  2    I  I  N  I  I    N  I  O  M  A    P  P  P  P  P    P  F  9
P  3  P  J  P    N  N  I  N  N    L  N  S  I  E    ø  ø  ø  ø  ø    ø  9  4
ø  5  ø  U  ø    O  O  A  O  O    A  O  I  N  M    V  V  V  V  V    V  4  2
V  5  V  5  V    Z  Z  M  Z  Z    M  Z  S  O  ø    3  3  3  3  3    3  2  X
3  U  3  4  3    T  T  G  T  T    G  T  X  Z  B    Q  Q  Q  Q  Q    Q  X  V
Q  V  Q  Y  Z    R  R  E  R  R    E  R  M  T  A    4  4  4  4  4    4  V  B
4  Z  4  5  4    S  S  W  S  S    W  S  K  R  U    X  X  X  X  X    X  B  B
X  K  X  Z  X    8  8  H  8  8    H  9  O  S  I    6  6  6  6  6    6  B  V
6  G  6  4  6    7  7  8  7  7    7  Z  9  Z  8    8  7  8  3  8    U  U  R
V  U  V  U  V    Y  Y  7  Y  Y    7  X  X  X  7    7  8  7  6  7    W  W
R  W  G  W  M    Y  Y  Y  Y  Y    X        X      Y  C  Y  Q  Y
```

16

D
M
W
K
9
B
J
J
L
H
Y
4
2

L
1
8
F
1
Z
5
X
6
H
4
4
Y

C
K
E
L
4
5
2
P
0
V
3
0
4
X
6
U
W

EXERCISE 4

```
1 7 4 3 4    L U U U L    L U L P L    H W L W U    1 J J J 1
1 J 1 6 1    7 4 3 6 0    B 6 B 6 B    B 6 B D B    U G K L F
0 9 9 9 0    0 9 0 0 0    3 8 1 6 3    H 5 H 5 H    H 5 H S H
V P B K V    3 2 2 2 3    3 2 3 4 3    3 4 6 0 6    Y M Y C Y
8 7 7 2 4    0 9 9 9 8    C K C Y C    P Z B Y Z    V 4 4 4 V
V 4 V S V    Q D Q L Q    6 B B B 6    6 B 6 G 6    C F X H V
8 9 8 7 8    D Z D Z C    2 7 5 1 9    G D C J Y    5 H H H 5
5 H 5 4 5    7 Z Z J 7    1 3 3 2 5    X V B B X    X X X P X
2 3 5 4 6    P L P J P    7 Z 7 Q 7    K M K D A    X T X N X
D B D G D    J U J 1 J    Z G Z 7 Z    W J W U W    F L F V F
R C H Z Y    R A R U R    R A R U R                 G Z G G G
S H S R S
```

EXERCISE 5

```
C B H H F    3 1 1 1 3    3 1 3 2 3    9 4 1 2 4    L P P P L
L P L F L    C L S Z J    0 9 9 9 0    0 9 0 Q 0    R 1 N F C
B 6 6 6 B    B 6 B D B    8 6 B 6 2    J 1 1 1 J    J 1 J U J
X I L B D    0 8 5 6 4    0 1 2 5 6    6 1 6 G 6    5 3 4 2 1
S H H H S    S H S I S    0 4 0 7 4    A T C P M    5 4 5 H 5
5 4 4 4 5    E S S J N    5 6 6 6 3    Z W X H P    8 7 7 7 8
8 7 8 3 8    W G Q K C    2 5 7 8 6    Q H O B F    H 5 5 5 H
H 5 H H H    G C B Q H    3 7 7 7 X    V 4 4 Z V    V 4 V U V
F 3 V 5 3    J B L Y I    X 6 6 6 V    R 6 X G X    X J J U P
V K G V Y    Q L X V O    X Y Y V U    R H G X K
```

EXERCISE 6

```
H M F V J    3 7 5 0 1    S H H H S    S H S R S    I K F H V
Y C E X P    0 9 9 9 0    0 9 0 2 0    8 2 5 4 1    X G G G X
X G X 6 X    4 6 4 2 7    F A A A F    F A F U F    3 0 6 7 8
R C J F H    B 6 6 6 B    B 6 B D B    A P I D Y    1 5 8 6 3
V G P I X    B 1 J 3 1    C Y 6 J X    H 5 5 5 H    H Y H S H
0 2 0 4 7    B J I P J    8 7 7 7 8    8 7 8 1 8    V V P N F
3 7 5 6 2    L Z P S L    L P L W L    2 8 0 3 5    J C L Q I
4 3 J 6 J    I P S L I    I S I A I    9 4 6 9 9    U 1 1 1 J
J 1 J U J    Y S L V Z    6 G G G 6    G 6 D 6      U H P F S
V 4 4 4 V    V W V U V    J T V V C
```

21. Method of Testing

a. The student should be provided with equipment for recording his own transmissions. Playback enables the student to check his timing, character formation, and general day-to-day progress. If recording equipment is not available, the instructor (or an advanced student) should copy the transmitted code, pointing out errors as noted.

b. The student should be seated at his position and permitted to adjust the sending key. If a coach is available, he should encourage the student to transmit for a few minutes without recording to become accustomed to the equipment. The coach should listen to the student's sending through his headset and make necessary corrections.

c. It is especially important to advise the student that operating speed must be achieved gradually.

For the first test, the student should practice sending a group of five characters in 8 seconds with a pause of 4 seconds before sending the next group of five characters, etc. Time these intervals accurately. If the student can send at this pace consistently, he will be able to pass a speed of five groups per minute in his first test. Through systematic sending practice of this type, student sense of timing improves as speed increases and tests are passed with minimum difficulty.

22. Method of Grading

a. To qualify at any given speed, a student must send continuously without error for 2 consecutive minutes during a 3-minute test.

b. The student tested should be informed of any errors made while sending and shown how best to correct his difficulties.

CHAPTER 4
STUDENT PROGRESS DATA

23. Student Progress

a. To determine student progress accurately, the code instructor must maintain individual records. The records may indicate chronologically the results of code sending and receiving tests, normally graded by the instructor. Occasionally, a student may correct his own paper when it is not used in qualifying the student for a particular speed.

b. An informational test can be designed in the *call-back* form. This test should not be identical in content with the standard qualifying test, because frequent identical tests will permit a student to memorize enough of the test to permit fill-in when he has missed small portions of the characters sent. After running the test for 5 minutes, the instructor should call back phonetically the characters he has sent—each student will correct his own copy. A test of this type should require no more than 20 minutes of class time to administer and correct. The student will count the number of groups he was able to copy correctly, and will then spend a reasonable time studying the type of error he made most frequently.

c. The results of call-back tests enable the instructor to diagnose accurately the particular difficulty delaying the individual's progress at any given speed. This type test is especially valuable when large classes, which necessitate automatic equipment, make personal contact impossible.

d. With this type of information available, the instructor is capable of interpreting student performance for a given speed in terms of any established standard.

24. Sending and Receiving Errors

a. *Dotting errors* usually occur at high-speed receiving levels and consist of confusing characters which differ from one another only in the number of dits contained in the signal. For example, H is frequently heard as S, B as D, and V as U. Distinguishing between these characters becomes more difficult as the speed of transmission increases, and

some students have difficulty in overcoming [ ] at high-speed receiving. The tendency to [ ] dotting errors should be brought to the atte[ ] of the student, and some form of remedial pr[ ] should be required of the student if the error[ ] tinue. This remedial practice may consist of s[ ] tapes of the more difficult characters placed [ ] together. For further practice, the student s[ ] send, 50 times, a character similar to the one [ ] gives him difficulty and then send the dif[ ] character 50 times. When the difference bet[ ] the two characters is thoroughly recognized [ ] student should insert the confusing charact[ ] characters in random groups of five. It w[ ] helpful for the student to listen to his own t[ ] mission of difficult characters if a recording c[ ] made of his sending practice.

b. Some students make an error which is [ ] monly known as *copying too close*. The ten[ ] to copy too quickly results in only part of the [ ] being heard before the character is written [ ] Copying an A for a W is an example of this mi[ ] When errors of this type are common in a stu[ ] copy, he should be encouraged to delay his res[ ] to the code signal. Good remedial practice [ ] sists of sending single characters with long p[ ] between signals. The student is required to [ ] until the signal is finished before writing the [ ] acter.

c. The receiving ability of some studen[ ] affected adversely by the advance from one [ ] to another. A student may be able to pas[ ] requirements for one speed but have an incre[ ] number of errors in every test at the next [ ] speed. It is detrimental to the student to p[ ] him to practice on a particular speed if he i[ ] capable of copying at least one-third of the ma[ ] correctly. His ability to copy at the next [ ] speed level will improve sharply if he is return[ ] the next lower speed for additional practice. [ ] tice at a fast character speed, but with longer sp[ ] between characters will also be helpful.

18

AGO

25. Progress Data

a. Graphs are intended to provide a basis for evaluating the performance of students at various speeds. Records of code learning frequently indicate student standing only in relation to these graphs.

b. It is important to relate a student's progress to that of other students under similar training conditions and with the same opportunities for learning.

c. Standards will be ineffective if they are ambiguous or based upon arbitrary requirements. Students should know what the standards are.

d. A student who passes any given speed as rapidly as, or in less time than, the first 25 percent of the group should be rated as a good student. It will be advantageous to assign a grading system to the four quarters of each class at each speed and rate the student accordingly.

26. Cumulative Code Practice Records

a. The family of curves shown in figure 9 represents a cumulative record of code learning from the beginning of practice through 15 gpm. These curves are based on the records of 200 men trained in basic code by the code-voice method with 4 hours of code practice per day.

b. The figures have a high degree of accuracy for any normal instructional situation, but it should be remembered that they resulted from factors existing at a specific school. A change in the aptitude of students, the method of teaching, and other factors will naturally tend to change the results. Instructors are encouraged to devise similar graphs or tables for their own classes. The only requirements are a record of the hours of practice a student has had and the number of groups he can copy correctly in a call-back test.

c. A family of curves, representing progress through all of the speeds taught in a code school, shows the student and the instructor where any man stands in relation to the entire group, and enables the instructor to evaluate individual student progress. For example, a student who had 50 hours of of code practice has just passed the 12 gpm test. By referring to the curve in figure 9, the instructor discovers that the student is doing as well as 38 percent of the students in the school. In the same number of practice hours, 14 percent passed 15 gpm, and 67 percent have passed 10 gpm. The student who has passed the 12-gpm test is better than the low average in learning to copy code.

d. Frequently the code instructor is interested in knowing how far a student should progress in a given number of hours. The information contained in figure 9 presents such information. The graph is intended primarily to show the code instructor what can be done with simple, accurate records. The code instructor will desire to collect similar data based on the conditions in his own classes. Com-

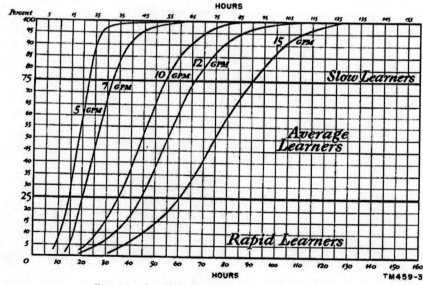

Figure 9. Cumulative hours required to pass 5 to 15 gpm.

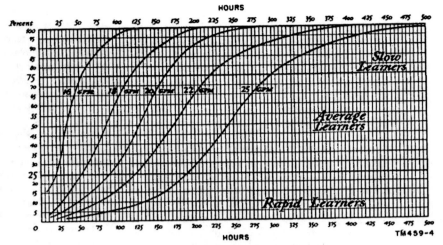

Figure 10. Cumulative hours required to pass 16 to 25 gpm.

parable teaching conditions should produce figures similar to the ones presented in this graph. If the graph data appear inaccurate after observation of approximately 500 students, a new graph should be plotted.

27. Learning Curves for Higher Speeds

Progress in learning to copy code above the 15-gpm level of code receiving is affected by factors not related to total practice hours. Dotting errors, copying too close, and the disruption which occurs when some students advance from one speed to the next, all tend to complicate the learning proc Training for high-speed operators should also clude other allied subjects not required by the l speed operator. For these reasons, the stude progress in learning to copy code at speeds fa that 18 gpm may not be comparable to his advai ment through the lower speeds. Notice that figure 10, the maximum hours are higher than tl shown in the curves at lower speeds, and that a men cannot qualify at 25 gpm even after 500 hc of practice. This is probably caused by s physiological factor rather than a lack of suffic: practice.

CHAPTER 5
TYPING

28. General

a. Many radio assignments require the operator to use touch typing. For example, fixed-station and high-speed operators usually learn to use the typewriter from the start of their training.

b. Special typewriters (fig. 11) have been designed for radio operators. The keyboard of such a typewriter differs slightly from that of a standard typewriter. On these typewriters, *all* numerals, including 1, are on the top row of keys and all letters are printed as capitals. An experienced typist will have no difficulty in adapting himself to minor changes on the keyboard.

c. The student should familiarize himself with the operation of the typewriter before he begins prac tice. The most important adjustments to the machine are margin stops, margin release,

carriage return, back spacer, line-space regulator, space bar, shift key, and ribbon mechanism. The proper method of inserting paper in the typewriter is important for smooth operation. Keep a supply of paper at the left side of the machine. After operating the paper release, pull the typed message from the roller with the right hand and with the left hand pick up a new sheet for insertion in the machine. Spin the platen knob with the right hand to start the new blank through the roller while the right arm is pulling the carriage into position for typing the first line of the next message or the continuation of the present message. Practice will result in smooth and skillful operation.

d. Learning to sit in front of the typewriter correctly from the beginning of practice will enable the operator to work for hours without fatigue. The

Figure 11. Portable typewriter.

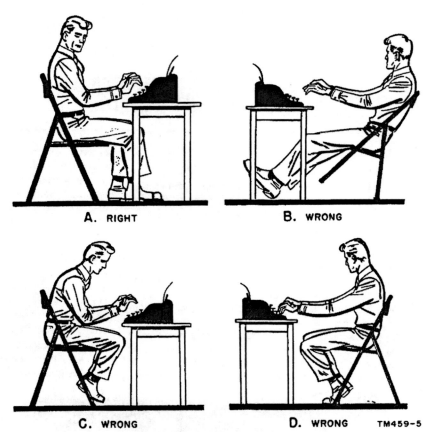

A. RIGHT   B. WRONG

C. WRONG   D. WRONG   TM459-5

Figure 12.   Right and wrong typing postures.

body should be erect and evenly balanced, and the arms should hang naturally without hugging the sides or extending outward at the elbows. Both feet should be flat on the floor. The forearms should be horizontal and the hands free to move at the wrist.

e. In A, figure 12, the student is seated correctly at the typewriter. His body is erect and well balanced, arms hang naturally and both feet are flat on the floor; in B the student will tire quickly. His leg muscles are strained in an effort to keep the chair balanced on two legs, and his body slumps down on the base of the spine. The man is seated too far from the keyboard and must stretch his arms to reach it. In C, the position shown is cramped and unnatural and will cause fatigue. The leg and abdominal muscles must strain to keep the body in this position. It is more restful to keep the feet flat on the floor. The effort required to reach the keyboard from the position shown in D will

tire the arm muscles quickly. Sit close enoug the typewriter to be comfortable and relaxe all times.

29. Keyboard Operation

a. When the student has a comfortable, rel position before the typewriter, his fingers shoul placed on the keys in the home position (fig. In the home position, the four fingers of the hand will cover the keys *ASDF* and the four fin of the right hand will cover *JKL;* These are guide keys for both hands, and the student sh learn the positions of the other letters of the board in relation to them. The fingers of l hands should always rest lightly on the home tion keys except when actually typing.

b. The keys should be struck with quick, sl strokes, but hammering or pounding the keys sh be avoided. The fingers should reach for the l and exert force from the wrist, not from the sho ers. The thumb of the right hand is used to operate the space bar. At the end of each typed line, the carriage is returned to the right by means of the carriage lever. The carriage lever is pushed by the left hand all the way to the margin stop. The motion of the lever will automatically turn the platen in position for the next line.

c. Practice is begun by placing the fingers on the guide keys in the home position. ASDF JKL; must be typed without looking at the keyboard. To learn the positions of the characters on the keyboard, the student must avoid looking at the keyboard while practicing. When the positions of the various characters on the keyboard become fixed in the student's mind, he will automatically strike the right keys. The student must strive for accuracy in early practice, and not be discouraged because he is unable to type rapidly. Gradually he attains speed as practice continues. During early practice, the keys are located by means of the keyboard diagram (fig. 13). When the student can automatically place his fingers on the guide

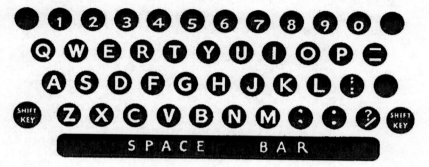

Figure 13. A type keyboard diagram.

keys and type the letters over and over without error, he is ready to begin the exercises in paragraph 30.

30. Typing Exercises

a. Typing drills should be prepared to enable students to acquire keyboard technique with minimum time and effort. The exercises shown below illustrate a method that may be used in instructing student typists with the typewriter keyboard. More extensive and repetitive exercises should be arranged for additional basic and advanced typing instructions. The method for the typist to gain speed on the typewriter is to practice sente containing all the letters of the alphabet. T should be written from 10 to 100 times. In d this, the typist should avoid spasmodic mot and should strike the keys in even time and equal force.

b. When students have attained the keyb technique, they should learn to coordinate ty while receiving the Morse character sounds musical tape using a superimposed beat car used to establish patterns of rhythm.

c. Before typing the following exercises, student will set the marginal stops and line s regulator and then insert the paper:

EXERCISE 1

```
ASDFG HJKL;  ASDFG HJKL;  ASDFG HJKL;  ASDFG HJKL;  ASDFG HJKL; ASDFG
ASK ASK ASK ASK ASK    ASK ASK ASK ASK ASK    ASK ASK ASK ASK ASK    ASK
LAD LAD LAD LAD LAD    LAD LAD LAD LAD LAD    LAD LAD LAD LAD LAD
ALL ALL ALL ALL ALL    ALL ALL ALL ALL ALL    ALL ALL ALL ALL ALL    ALL
SAD SAD SAD SAD SAD    SAD SAD SAD SAD SAD    SAD SAD SAD SAD SAD    SAD SAD
GAS GAS GAS GAS GAS    GAS GAS GAS GAS GAS    GAS GAS GAS GAS GAS    GAS GAS
ADD ADD ADD ADD ADD    ADD ADD ADD ADD ADD    ADD ADD ADD ADD ADD
FALL FALL FALL FALL FALL    FALL FALL FALL FALL FALL    FALL FALL FALL FALL
ASKS ASKS ASKS ASKS ASKS    ASKS ASKS ASKS ASKS ASKS    ASKS ASKS ASKS ASKS
ALAS ALAS ALAS ALAS ALAS    ALAS ALAS ALAS ALAS ALAS    ALAS ALAS ALAS ALAS
```

EXERCISE 2

```
FUR FUR FUR FUR FUR    FUR FUR FUR FUR FUR    FUR FUR FUR FUR FUR    FUR FUR
RUG RUG RUG RUG RUG    RUG RUG RUG RUG RUG    RUG RUG RUG RUG RUG    RUG
HUG HUG HUG HUG HUG    HUG HUG HUG HUG HUG    HUG HUG HUG HUG HUG
JUG JUG JUG JUG JUG    JUG JUG JUG JUG JUG    JUG JUG JUG JUG JUG    JUG JUG JUG
HUM HUM HUM HUM HUM    HUM HUM HUM HUM HUM    HUM HUM HUM HUM HUM
RUM RUM RUM RUM RUM    RUM RUM RUM RUM RUM    RUM RUM RUM RUM RUM
FGHNJ RUFGH MJRUF GHMJR UFGHM    JRUFG HMJRU FHJUG MRFGJ UMUGJ
MRMGU JHFMU GUJHF RMHRM HFRMG    UJJFU MGUJH FRUHG FHRFM GUGJJ
FJGRH UMFJG RHUMF JGRHU MFJHR    JUUFG GMHRM FJHRJ UUFMG UHGMJ
FURJM JHFUU JMGHF RHUMF FUUGH    FGGHG GGJMG MMGHR UHJFG FMRJG
```

EXERCISE 3

```
VERY VERY VERY VERY VERY    VERY VERY VERY VERY VERY    VERY VERY VERY
DUTY DUTY DUTY DUTY DUTY    DUTY DUTY DUTY DUTY DUTY    DUTY DUTY DUTY
HUNT HUNT HUNT HUNT HUNT    HUNT HUNT HUNT HUNT HUNT    HUNT HUNT
BUNK BUNK BUNK BUNK BUNK    BUNK BUNK BUNK BUNK BUNK    BUNK BUNK BUNK
RUDDY RUDDY RUDDY RUDDY    RUDDY RUDDY RUDDY RUDDY RUDDY    RUDDY
```

EXERCISE 4

```
OIL OIL OIL OIL OIL    OIL OIL OIL OIL OIL    OIL OIL OIL OIL OIL    OIL OIL OIL OIL OIL
SEW SEW SEW SEW SEW    SEW SEW SEW SEW SEW    SEW SEW SEW SEW SEW    SEW
CIVIL CIVIL CIVIL CIVIL CIVIL    CIVIL CIVIL CIVIL CIVIL CIVIL    CIVIL CIVIL CIVIL
CONVEX CONVEX CONVEX CONVEX    CONVEX CONVEX CONVEX    CONVEX CONVEX CONVEX CONVEX
CREST CREST CREST CREST CREST    CREST CREST CREST CREST CREST    CREST
BLINK BLINK BLINK BLINK BLINK    BLINK BLINK BLINK BLINK BLINK    BLINK
```

EXERCISE 5

PALMS PALMS PALMS PALMS PALMS   PALMS PALMS PALMS PALMS PALMS   PALMS
SQUAW SQUAW SQUAW SQUAW SQUAW   SQUAW SQUAW SQUAW SQUAW SQUAW
QUICK QUICK QUICK QUICK QUICK   QUICK QUICK QUICK QUICK QUICK   QUICK
ZERO ZERO ZERO ZERO ZERO   ZERO ZERO ZERO ZERO ZERO   ZERO ZERO ZERO ZERO
ZIGZAG ZIGZAG ZIGZAG ZIGZAG ZIGZAG   ZIGZAG ZIGZAG ZIGZAG ZIGZAG ZIGZAG
XVT45 XVT45 XVT45 XVT45 XVT45   XVT45 XVT45 XVT45 XVT45 XVT45   XVT45 XVT45

EXERCISE 6

A1S2D A1S2D A1S2D A1S2D A1S2D   A1S2D A1S2D A1S2D A1S2D A1S2D   A1S2D A1S2D
3F461 3F461 3F461 3F461 3F461   3F461 3F461 3F461 3F461 3F461   3F461 3F461 3F461 3F461
5H6J7 5H6J7 5H6J7 5H6J7 5H6J7   5H6J7 5H6J7 5H6J7 5H6J7 5H6J7   5H6J7 5H6J7 5H6J7
K8L90 K8L90 K8L90 K8L90 K8L90   K8L90 K8L90 K8L90 K8L90 K8L90   K8L90 K8L90 K8L90
J0H98 J0H98 J0H98 J0H98 J0H98   J0H98 J0H98 J0H98 J0H98 J0H98   J0H98 J0H98 J0H98 J0H98
G1F23 G1F23 G1F23 G1F23 G1F23   G1F23 G1F23 G1F23 G1F23 G1F23   G1F23 G1F23 G1F23
F4J65 F4J65 F4J65 F4J65 F4J65   F4J65 F4J65 F4J65 F4J65 F4J65   F4J65 F4J65 F4J65 F4J65
H5G67 H5G67 H5G67 H5G67 H5G67   H5G67 H5G67 H5G67 H5G67 H5G67   H5G67 H5G67

CHAPTER 6
SEMIAUTOMATIC KEY

31. Use

The semiautomatic key, also known as the *Vibroplex*, or *bug*, is used chiefly in fixed stations where operators are required to send for relatively long periods of time.

32. Operation

a. In sending with the bug, the thumb presses the *dit paddle* (fig. 14) to the right and the index finger forms dahs by pressing the knob to the left. The key will send successive dits when the paddle is held to the right. One dit or a series may be sent, depending on how long the thumb pressure is maintained against the paddle. One dah is formed every time the knob is pressed to the left. Dahs must be sent individually.

b. During sending, the hand pivots at the wrist, and the hand and arm motion is horizontal.

33. Key Adjustment

a. Best operation of the semiautomatic key will be obtained when it is adjusted to send dits and spaces of equal length. Locate the parts in figure 14 when adjusting the key. The top view in figure 14 shows the section of the key between the dah contact adjusting screw and the front stop screw.

b. Before adjusting the semiautomatic key, examine it for mechanical and electrical defects. *First*, make certain that both *dit and dah contacts* are clean and in perfect alinement with the faces parallel. *Second*, make sure that the *lever pivoting screw* is loose enough to permit the lever to move freely. Signals will sound unsteady if it is too loose. *Third*, examine all supporting parts to make certain that they are firm and steady. *Fourth*, make certain that stop screws and locknuts are tight. *Fifth*, inspect the cord and plug for short circuits or loose connections.

c. Adjust the key as follows:

(1) Place the key on a level surface.

(2) Adjust the *back stop screw* until the reed lightly touches the *deadener*. Then tigh the *locknut*.

(3) Adjust the *front stop screw* until the sep: tion between the end of this screw the reed is approximately .015 i (Approx 10 pp of this manual inse between the screw and lever will s as a convenient guide.) Then tigh the locknut. A greater separation is missible if the operator prefers more l movement.

(4) Operate the dit paddle to the right. I the lever in this position and stop vibration of the reed. Adjust the *contact adjusting screw* until the dit tacts just meet. This important adj ment determines whether the dits wil too heavy, too light, or perfect. adjustment must be made without fle the *contact spring*. Tighten the lock on the dit contact adjusting screw with disturbing the adjustment.

(5) If the dits are too fast, move the *we* located on the reed, in the directio the deadener. If the dits are too s move the same weight in the oppo direction.

(6) Adjust the *dah contact adjusting screw* clearance approximately the thicknes the cover on a Department of the A field or technical manual.

(7) Adjust the *dit retractive* and *dah ten* springs for the most comfortable operat

d. Do not readjust the dit contact adjus screw unless a complaint is received or unless are certain that your dits are too heavy or light. Never change the back stop screw adj ment when the bug is correctly adjusted. It sh not be necessary to change the front stop s adjustment. However, if the locknut on the f stop screw should become loose, it will be neces to readjust the dit contact adjusting screw. I

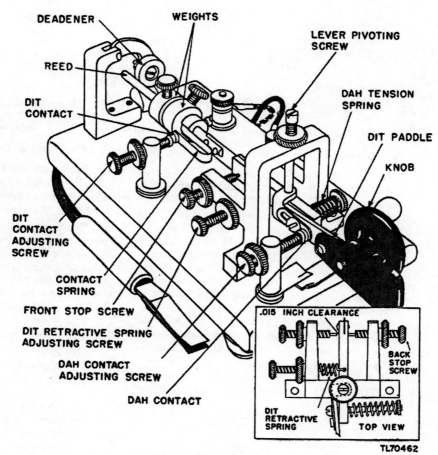

DEADENER

WEIGHTS

LEVER PIVOTING SCREW

REED

DAH TENSION SPRING

DIT CONTACT

DIT PADDLE

KNOB

DIT CONTACT ADJUSTING SCREW

CONTACT SPRING

FRONT STOP SCREW

DIT RETRACTIVE SPRING ADJUSTING SCREW

DAH CONTACT ADJUSTING SCREW

DAH CONTACT

.015 INCH CLEARANCE

BACK STOP SCREW

DIT RETRACTIVE SPRING

TOP VIEW

TL70462

Figure 14. Semiautomatic key.

dah contact adjusting screw is too close, the dah contacts will remain shorted.

e. A change in the position of the weight for the speed of dits or a change in the tension of the retractive and dah springs to suit the individual's requirements will not throw the *bug* out of proper adjustment.

f. If the adjustment instructions are followed carefully, the *bug* will make 25 or more dits before stopping. The first 12 to 15 dits will be practically perfect with the dits and spaces equal.

g. The *bug* is designed to make sending easy rather than fast, and perfect control of the key is far more important than speed. Be especially careful to send dits accurately. Not all radio operators have equally sensitive hearing, and careless sending on the semiautomatic key will not be understood.

CHAPTER 7
RADIO OPERATOR TRAINING

34. General

a. When the student can receive and distinguish code characters, he should be trained in allied subjects to qualify him as a radio operator.

b. Training in radiotelegraph procedures (message format, prosigns, log and number sheets, net operating procedures, etc., see ACP 124 (B)), gradually should be combined with instructions as code speed progresses. After the student has reached a qualifying speed, he should be trained to operate in a simulated radio net and become familiar with all phases of station practices.

c. Instructions on various types of radio sets (methods of installation and operation together with such necessary electronic fundamentals) should be included in student training.

d. Supplementary training should include—
   (1) General instructions in communications (ACP 121 (C)).
   (2) Regulations and procedures of radio transmission security (ACP 122 (B)).
   (3) Operation of cryptographic devices not requiring cryptologic clearance (equipment manual).
   (4) Radiotelephone operation and procedures (ACP 125 (B)).
   (5) Visual signaling (ACP 118(D) and FM 21–60).
   (6) Communication center operation (FM 11–17).
   (7) Defense against jamming (FM 11–151).
   (8) Preventive maintenance (equipment manual).

35. Operator's Duties

a. Radio operators must always use the] scribed procedures; unauthorized changes in] cedures will cause confusion, reduce reliability speed, and decrease communication security.

b. Before a radio operator takes over a r: circuit, he should check for special orders conc ing his circuit and awaiting messages, change: radio organization, and other pertinent matt He should determine also that the radio set i: efficient operating condition and properly tunec the assigned frequency.

c. Radio communication will be improved if following general rules are observed:
   (1) Listen in before transmitting to av interference.
   (2) Make only the minimum transmiss necessary to maintain net contact anc clear traffic.
   (3) Send call signs clearly and accuratel:
   (4) Transmit at speeds not faster than tl of the slowest operator in the net.
   (5) Reply promptly to all transmissions req ing a reply.
   (6) Operate with minimum power requirec maintain communications with all tions in the net.
   (7) Conform strictly to prescribed radio] cedure and regulations for maintaii transmission security.
   (8) Write out and rehearse radio mess: before going on the air.

APPENDIX
REFERENCES

1. Publications

AR 320–50	Authorized Abbreviations.
ACP 118(D)	Visual Call Sign Book.
ACP 121(C)	CM.
ACP 121(C)–1	Communication Instruction, General.
ACP 122(B)	CM.
ACP 124(B)	CM.
ACP 126	CM.
ACP 129A	Communication Instructions, Visual Signaling Procedure.
ACP 131	Communication Instructions —Operating Signals.
ACP 167	CM.
FM 21–5	Military Training.
FM 21–6	Techniques of Military Instruction.
FM 21–30	Military Symbols.
FM 21–60	Visual Signals.
DA Pam 108–1	Index of Army Motion Pictures, Film Strips, Slides, and Phono-Recordings.
DA Pam 310–1	Index of Administrative Publications.
DA Pam 310–3	Index of Training Publications.
DA Pam 310–4	Index of Technical Manuals, Technical Regulations, Technical Bulletins, Supply Bulletins, Lubrication Orders, and Modification Work Orders.
DA Pam 310–5	Military Publications Index of Graphic Training Aids and Devices.
SR 320–5–1	Dictionary of United States Army Terms.
TM 11–390	Signal Lamp Equipments EE–80 and EE–80–A.
TM 11–391	Signal Lamp Equipment EE–84.
TM 11–392	Signal Lamp Equipment SE–11.
TM 11–437A	Code Training Set AN/GSC–T1A.
TM 11–2548	Magnetic Wire Recorder and Reproducer (GE Models 50A and 51).
TM 11–2584	Sound Recorder-Reproducer RD–87A/U.
TM 11–2093	Code Practice Equipments EE–94–F and EE–95–F.

2. Training Films

TF 11–1694	Radio Operator Training— Technique of Hand Sending.
TF 11–1695	Radio Operator Training— Rhythm, Speed, and Accuracy in Hand Sending.

INDEX

[AG 311 (31 Jul 57)]

By order of the Secretaries of the Army and the Air Force:

MAXWELL D. TAYLOR,
General, United States Army,
Chief of Staff.

Official:
HERBERT M. JONES,
Major General, United States Army,
The Adjutant General.

Official:
J. L. TARR,
Colonel, United States Air Force,
Air Adjutant General.

THOMAS D. WHITE,
Chief of Staff, United States Air Force.

Distribution:
  Active Army:
    ASA
    CNGB
    Technical Stf, DA
    Technical Stf Bd
    USA Arty Bd
    USA Armor Bd
    USA Inf Bd
    USA Air Def Bd
    USA Abn & Elct Bd
    USA Avn Bd
    USA Armor Bd Test Sec
    USA Air Def Bd Test Sec
    USA Arctic Test Bd
    USCONARC
    US ARADCOM
    OS Maj Comd
    MDW
    Armies
    Corps
    Div
    USATC
    Ft & Camp
    Svc Colleges
    Br Svc Sch
    Gen Depots
    Sig Sec, Gen Depots
    Sig Depots
    Fld Comd, AFSWP
    Engr Maint Cen
    Army Pictorial Cen

    WRAMC
    AFIP
    AMS
    Port of Emb (OS)
    Trans Terminal Comd
    Army Terminals
    OS Sup Agcy
    USA Sig Pub Agcy
    USA Sig Comm Engr Agcy
    USA Comm Agcy
    TASSA
    USA White Sands Sig Agcy
    USA Sig Eqp Sup Agcy
    Yuma Test Sta
    USA Elct PG
    Sig Fld Maint Shops
    Sig Lab
    Mil Dist
    JBUSMC
    Units org under fol TOE:
    11–7
    11–16
    11–57
    11–127
    11–128
    11–500
    11–557
    11–587
    11–592
    11–597

NG: State AG; units—same as Active Army.
USAR: None.
For explanation of abbreviations used, see AR 320–50.

CPSIA information can be obtained
at www.ICGtesting.com
Printed in the USA
LVOW09s1041121117
555989LV00032B/1462/P